GOOD LUCK
BABY OWLS

Written by **Giles Milton**

Illustrated by **Alexandra Milton**

Boxer Books

Frost-coated silence,
a chill winter's night.
All is quiet in the
big dark barn.

All is quiet
except for a squeak.
A *squeakity-squeak* in the
big dark barn.

"Daddy, Daddy, Daddy!"
squeak two baby owls.

"Please, please, Daddy, Daddy,
can we learn how to fly?"

"Not yet," says Daddy. "You're far too small. You must wait for the spring when your wings will be strong!"

"But look, Daddy, Daddy," squeak two baby owls.

"We can both flap our wings.
Oh, please can we fly?"

"You must eat all your food,"
says kind Daddy Owl. "You need
to be strong to fly to the sky."

Day after day and week after week, they eat and they stretch and they flap their small wings.

"Tonight," says Daddy, "we shall learn how to fly! Tonight we shall learn how to fly to the sky."

High on a rafter sit two frightened owls.
Below, far below, is the far-away ground.

Above, far above, is the far-away sky.

"We're scared!" cry the owls.
"It's a long way to fall."

"Lean forward and flap,"
says strong Daddy Owl.

"We did it! We did it!
We learned how to fly!"
"I'm proud," says Daddy.
"So, how did it feel?"

"The sky is so empty,
so silent and clean ...
like floating in magic ...
can we do it again?"

"You can fly to the heavens, you can fly to the moon.

Good luck, baby owls— but fly back soon!"

For Philippe

G.M & A.M

First published in Great Britain in 2012
by Boxer Books Limited
www.boxerbooks.com

Text copyright © 2012 Giles Milton
Illustrations copyright © 2012 Alexandra Milton
The rights of Giles Milton to be identified as the author and
Alexandra Milton as the illustrator of this work have been asserted by them
in accordance with the Copyright, Designs and Patents Act, 1988.

The illustrations were prepared using collage, colour pencil and ink.

ISBN 978-1-907967-29-0

1 3 5 7 9 10 8 6 4 2

Printed in China

All of our papers are sourced from managed forests and renewable resources.